WAFFLES

THE PUPPY PLACE

Don't miss any of the other stories by Ellen Miles!

THE PUPPY PLACE

WAFFLES

ELLEN MILES

SCHOLASTIC INC.

For all the kids who have told me that the Puppy Place books
helped them learn to love reading!

Copyright © 2024 by Ellen Miles
Cover art by Tim O'Brien
Original cover design by Steve Scott

ISBN 978-1-339-01227-8

10 9 8 7 6 5 4 3 2 1   24 25 26 27 28

Printed in the U.S.A.   40
First printing 2024

CHAPTER ONE

"Really? You're hungry again?" Maria's dad shook his head as he reached for his wallet.

Lizzie Peterson and her best friend, Maria Santiago, grinned at each other. It wasn't that they were hungry, exactly. Just a half hour earlier they'd inhaled pumpkin-spice waffles slathered in sweet, fluffy whipped cream. But they were at the county fair! And there were so many yummy things to eat. Corn dogs, fries, and BBQ sandwiches. Onion rings! Apple cider doughnuts! Cotton candy! All the smells blended together into one delicious cloud.

Lizzie loved the fair. She'd gone every fall for as

long as she could remember, and Mom had told her that she'd even loved it as a toddler—the age her brother, the Bean, was now—when she still sometimes rode in a stroller. Lizzie loved the midway, the long, wide walking path lined with stalls selling everything from socks to crystals, burritos to smoothies. Oh, and the games! Lizzie loved the games, where you could win rainbow glow sticks or a giant stuffie. But those weren't even the best part of the fair. What she loved most were all the animals, the ones who spent the fair in stalls at one end of the midway. These were the best of the best farm animals, brought here by their owners from all over the region. Oxen as big as Volkswagen Beetles, tiny pink piglets, beautiful chickens in every color of the rainbow, goats and geese and horses and even llamas. Lizzie loved meeting curly-haired sheep; watching 4-H kids in clean white shirts lead their calves into the judging ring; and counting baby bunnies in their hutches. Lizzie knew that every single one of these animals was treated with love and care, and that made her happy.

"Wait," said Maria now. She held up a hand. "Before we eat anything else, maybe we should go on that ride."

Lizzie gulped. She knew which ride Maria was talking about. This wasn't the tame carousel or the Ferris wheel that stopped when you were way up at the top and left you rocking in the breeze, looking out over the whole fair.

No, the ride Maria wanted to go on was called the Octopus, and it whirled and twirled and threw you upside down and sideways and . . .

"Um," said Lizzie. She knew Maria was right: It was better to wait to eat. There was no way she was going to ride on the Octopus after having a cup of chili with cheese or a large order of sweet potato fries. That would definitely be a mistake. Actually, in Lizzie's mind it was a mistake to go on the Octopus at all. But if Maria really, really wanted her to . . .

"How about if you and I go on that one together?" Mr. Santiago said to Maria. Lizzie shot Maria's dad a grateful look. She could tell that he had guessed the truth: Lizzie was afraid of scary rides. "Lizzie and your mom can go check out the pony pull."

Maria's mom put her arm through Lizzie's. "Great idea," she said. "Lizzie can tell me all about what's happening."

Maria's mom was blind. She had the most wonderful guide dog, Simba, who sat at her side at that very moment, waiting patiently for the humans to make a decision.

"I love the pony pull!" said Lizzie. She remembered it from last year. The "ponies" were actually huge horses, all decked out in beautiful harnesses covered with shiny silver badges. These were horses that were meant to pull plows or heavy trucks full of logs. They were so strong! For the contest, they took turns hauling a big flat-bottomed sled (called a "boat") covered with concrete slabs. Each time they made it through a round, helpers added more weight to the boat, using the kind of machinery that Lizzie's other younger brother, Charles, loved to watch.

Lizzie found seats for herself and Mrs. Santiago, and they settled in on the bleachers just as the last round of action began. A woman made announcements over a crackly loudspeaker, telling the crowd which handlers and which ponies were still competing in the final round. "And this time they'll be pulling five thousand, two hundred pounds," she finished. "Let's welcome our first team, Sarah Owens with Pete and Bob!"

Lizzie and Mrs. Santiago joined in the applause. "Wow," Lizzie said, leaning over to whisper in Mrs. Santiago's ear. "The horses are enormous. One of them is brown, and the other is white. And their handler is—well, she's not big. She's practically, like, my size!" Lizzie watched, fascinated, as the young woman moved the horses into place, backing them up so her teammate could hook up the boat and holding them steady so they wouldn't pull too soon or unevenly.

Lizzie remembered that the pony handlers often yelled and cracked whips to get the horses to do what they wanted them to do. Not this woman. She spoke in a soft voice and made small movements with her hands that the horses seemed to understand and respond to right away. Lizzie explained this all to Mrs. Santiago, then leaned forward, watching closely, as the woman dropped her hand and gave a soft one-word command. The horses surged forward and the sled slid along the soft, sandy soil. When they stopped, unable to pull any farther, a man ran up, checked the length of their pull with a tape measure, and hollered out a number. The crowd applauded and cheered.

"That'll take the blue ribbon," Lizzie heard the man next to her say.

After three other teams had competed (with lots of loud yelling on the part of the handlers), there was a brief pause while the judges looked over the figures. Then the loudspeaker crackled. "Blue ribbon goes to Sarah Owens with Pete and Bob."

The young woman ran into the ring to grab her ribbon, grinned at the crowd, then dashed off. Lizzie laughed. "I guess she has somewhere else to be," she told Mrs. Santiago. "She looks happy with her blue ribbon, but she's in a hurry." Lizzie and Mrs. Santiago clapped for the woman even though she'd left the ring, then they stayed on for the second- and third-place winners as well.

"That was so cool," Lizzie said as they got up and headed back to the midway to meet up with Maria and her dad. "That handler Sarah Owens was amazing. I wish I could have that kind of control over Buddy, not to mention some of the puppies we've fostered." Lizzie knew she was a good dog trainer for her age, but she also knew that she had a lot to learn. She was lucky to be able to practice on all sorts of dogs, since her family fostered puppies who needed homes. (Sweet, cute Buddy was the only one they'd kept for good.)

"You Petersons do such a great job with your puppies," said Mrs. Santiago. "And you always find them the best homes, too."

"Speaking of puppies," said Lizzie. "I noticed there was a really cute purple puppy stuffie as a prize at this basketball-toss game we passed before. Maria would love it."

"Then let's go try to win it for her," said Mrs. Santiago. "Lead on!"

A few minutes later, Lizzie stood at the basketball-toss booth, getting ready to take one more shot. She'd missed by a mile on her first two, but she was determined to get the ball into the basket this time. She held the ball carefully, getting herself set into position. She lifted the ball. She aimed. She tossed—just as something banged into her elbow, causing the ball to fly sideways, straight into the man who was in charge of the booth. "Oof!" he said.

"Sorry!" Lizzie frowned as she turned to see who had jostled her. Then she gasped. "Well, hello," she said. "Who are you?" She stared down at the most adorable fluffy white puppy, who immediately jumped up, touching her paws lightly on Lizzie's hip. The puppy grinned and tossed her flappy ears. Her black eyes sparkled mischievously.

Hi, friend! Isn't this fun? I'm having the greatest time.

Lizzie glanced up and down the midway, looking for the puppy's owner.

But nobody called her.

Nobody stepped forward to claim her.

"Uh-oh," said Lizzie.

CHAPTER TWO

"What's going on?" asked Mrs. Santiago. "Shh, shh, it's okay, Simba."

Simba let out a low whimper as the white puppy bounced over to him, went into a deep play bow with her little tail wagging like mad, then jumped up to pat her paw on the big, dignified dog's nose.

"It's a puppy," Lizzie told Mrs. Santiago. "She's trying to get Simba to play, but he won't."

As usual, Lizzie noted, Simba behaved perfectly. His guide-dog training kept him sitting absolutely still at Mrs. Santiago's side as he watched the puppy's antics. He would have loved to play—Lizzie could tell that by the way his ears perked up and his tail twitched ever so slightly. And this puppy was doing everything in her power to tempt him. But Simba didn't budge.

"Good boy," said Mrs. Santiago, patting Simba's head. She reached out to feel for the puppy. "Oooh, such soft and fluffy curly hair!" she said as she stroked the puppy's ears. "Poodle?"

"Exactly what I was thinking!" said Lizzie. She laughed as she watched the poodle wriggle and dance, pushing against Mrs. Santiago's hand. "She's beautiful, pure white like a cloud. Maybe six months old? A standard poodle, probably. She's big but not full grown." Lizzie glanced at the man behind the counter. He was spinning a basketball on the tip of one finger as he waited for more customers. "Is this your puppy?" Lizzie asked.

He shrugged and shook his head. "Nope," he

said. "But I'm sure her owners are nearby. What do her tags say?"

Lizzie bent down for a closer look and felt her stomach lurch. "No collar!" she said. "Cutie, where do you belong?" The puppy just grinned up at her and offered a paw for a shake. Lizzie looked up and down the midway again. Throngs of happy fair-goers strolled by, eating fried food and ice-cream cones, laughing and talking. Nobody even glanced at the puppy.

"What do we do now?" Lizzie asked Mrs. Santiago. Lizzie was used to taking care of pup-pies, but this situation was a little overwhelming. So many people! So many animals! So many sights and sounds and smells! *And* a lost puppy.

"Well, for starters, let's take a deep breath," said Mrs. Santiago. "No need to panic. It's just a lost puppy, not the first time you've dealt with that, eh?" She smiled at Lizzie, and Lizzie immediately felt more relaxed. It was true; Lizzie's family had dealt with several lost puppies. She knew what steps to take—she just needed to calm herself down and remember them.

"Hey! What's going on? Who's this? Where'd you get the puppy? Whose is she?" Maria ran up to them and got down on her knees to say hello to the happy, squirming pup. "Look at you! Who's the fluffiest?" she murmured as she let the puppy sniff her hand, then climb into her arms.

"I should have figured," said Mr. Santiago, smiling as he joined them. "Leave Lizzie for five minutes, and when you come back she'll have a new puppy for you to meet."

Maria laughed. "You really are kind of a puppy magnet," she said, grinning up at Lizzie. "But where did this one come from?"

"That's what we're trying to figure out," said Lizzie. "Her owners don't seem to be anywhere nearby. I think we should walk up and down the midway with her and see if anybody recognizes her."

"Sounds good to me," said Maria, "as long as we can stop at that burrito place. Riding that Octopus gave me an appetite!"

Mr. Santiago groaned and held his stomach. "Not me," he said. "Kind of the opposite, actually."

They headed up the midway, past the Whac-A-Mole game, past the bumper-sticker stand, past three onion-ring spots and two chili-dog sellers and a stand full of paintings on velvet: tigers and puppies and mountain scenes all jumbled together. The puppy trotted along at Lizzie's side, bouncing up once in a while as if to make sure Lizzie didn't forget her.

This is fun! When do we meet up with my person?

Lizzie couldn't help smiling down at the puppy. She was so exuberant, so full of energy. She bounced along as if she were on springs and shook her head so that her floppy ears flipped and flapped happily. *Somebody must love this puppy,* Lizzie thought. *Somebody must be missing her.*

"Here!" said Maria, stopping at a turquoise food truck strung with white fairy lights. "Don't these burritos look fantastic?"

Lizzie shook her head. "I guess I'm not hungry," she said. All she could think about was how awful she would feel if she had lost a puppy like this one. "But you go ahead," she urged her friend. Lizzie stood waiting while Maria and her mom ordered. She looked up and down the midway and checked each face that went by. Why wasn't anybody stepping up with a cry of relief? *My puppy! There she is!* Lizzie could just hear it. But nobody stopped.

"Why don't you and your mom sit down here to eat?" Maria's dad suggested to Maria, pointing to a picnic table. "Lizzie and I will keep moving. Maybe we can find the fair's offices and have an announcement made."

"Great idea!" said Lizzie. "Like when they announce lost children." She patted her thigh, and the puppy—who had been gazing at Maria's burrito—popped up to join her. She followed Lizzie as Lizzie followed Mr. Santiago through the crowds toward a cluster of buildings near the Home and Garden Hall, where pies and cakes, quilts and woodworking projects, jams and jellies and homegrown veggies were all on display, waiting to be judged. Lizzie kept expecting the puppy to run off, looking for her people—but she stuck right by Lizzie's side as if the hustle and bustle of the fair was too much for her.

"Here we go," said Mr. Santiago, pointing to a

sign above a doorway. FAIRGROUND ADMINISTRATION, it said.

Lizzie felt relief wash over her. The people here would help them. They would make an announcement, and soon this adorable puppy would be reunited with her owners.

Mr. Santiago pushed at the door. "Oh, no," he said. "It's locked. They're closed."

Lizzie gulped. "Now what?" she asked.

CHAPTER THREE

Maria's dad looked down at the puppy, who had not left Lizzie's side for a second. "To be honest, I'm not sure what to do next," he said slowly. "She sure seems attached to you."

Lizzie reached down to ruffle the puppy's floppy ears. "Well, I like her, too," she said. The puppy gazed up at her with a trusting look.

I know you'll help me! I can just tell.

"But," Lizzie went on. "Somebody must really be missing this dog. She's not a stray, that's for sure. She's well-fed and healthy, and look at her coat! She's been professionally groomed recently. That's called a puppy cut. When she's older, they'll probably give her more of a fancy poodle cut." Lizzie admired the puppy. She really was adorable. And smart. Out of all the people at the fair, Lizzie was the one this pup had picked to glom on to. Somehow, she seemed to know that Lizzie Peterson was a puppy person.

"Let's go back and find the others," said Mr. Santiago. "Who knows? Maybe we'll run into her owners along the way."

They walked back down the midway. Instead of looking at the games and the food and all the brightly colored toys and tees for sale, now Lizzie looked at the people. Wasn't anyone trying to find their puppy? But nobody even seemed to notice the fluffy white pup prancing along beside Lizzie. They just ate their corn dogs and played the basketball toss and bought key chains and T-shirts.

"Any luck?" asked Mrs. Santiago when Lizzie and Mr. Santiago joined her and Maria. "I didn't hear any announcements."

"The offices seem to be closed for the night," said Mr. Santiago. He sighed. "I have to admit, I'm not sure what else we can do."

"Well, we can't just leave her here," said Lizzie. She couldn't stand to think of this cutie wandering the fair by herself. She shrugged and held out her hands. "So obviously, I'm going to have to take her home with me."

"Obviously!" said Maria, grinning. She gave Lizzie a high five. "I saw that coming."

"Shouldn't you ask your parents first?" Mr. Santiago asked.

"In a case like this, I think they'll understand," said Lizzie. "We can call them on the way home."

"Let's walk up and down the midway one more time," suggested Mr. Santiago. "But to tell the truth, I'm ready to go pretty soon. My feet are tired and I don't think I can go on another ride."

Maria agreed. "The Octopus was enough for me," she said.

"And after that burrito, I can't eat another thing," said Mrs. Santiago. "Sounds like we're all ready to go."

They strolled up the midway as far as the rides area, then back down again to where it ended at the animal barns. The puppy stuck close to Lizzie, bouncing along as happily as ever.

"Look at her," said Maria. "She's as white and fluffy as the whipped cream on those waffles we ate."

"That's the perfect name for her," Lizzie said.

"What, Whipped Cream?" asked Maria.

"No, Waffles!" Lizzie laughed. "We can call her that, just for now. I'm sure she's got another name, but—you know—as long as we have her . . ." She leaned down and scritched the puppy between the ears. "How about it, Waffles?" she asked. The puppy wagged her tail and let out a few happy yips.

Whatever you say, friend!

Lizzie laughed again. This was one of the happiest, friendliest puppies she'd ever met. If it turned out that they had to find her a new home, it wouldn't be hard at all. Who wouldn't love Waffles? Lizzie was already wishing she could keep this puppy herself—but she knew the rule. Her parents had repeated it often enough: "Not if you want to keep fostering puppies," they said every time she and Charles begged to make a foster puppy part of the family. "One permanent puppy is plenty."

Lizzie knew they were right—but it didn't stop her from falling in love with every puppy they fostered.

"Well, I guess that's it," said Mr. Santiago,

taking one last look around before they crossed the little footbridge over to the parking lot. "Waffles seems ready to leave the fair, too."

Lizzie couldn't believe how this pup had stuck beside her. No leash, no collar, just—what? Trust?

Mrs. Santiago seemed to read Lizzie's mind. "I have a feeling that Waffles knows a friend when she sees one," she said as they climbed into the car.

Waffles settled down between Maria and Lizzie in the backseat while Simba made himself comfortable by Mrs. Santiago's feet up front. For a big dog, he could squeeze into the tiniest space—as long as he was near his person.

Maria and Lizzie petted Waffles. "She's so soft," said Maria. "And she seems so smart and funny. How can your parents resist? She won't cause any trouble at all."

"Oh, no!" said Lizzie. "Don't say that! Don't jinx me!"

"What do you mean?" Maria asked.

Lizzie laughed. "It's just that every time somebody says that about one of our foster puppies—that they won't be any trouble—they turn out to be major trouble."

She stroked Waffles's floppy ears and kissed her on the nose. "But that's not going to happen with you, is it, Waffles?"

Waffles looked at Lizzie, and for just a moment the puppy's eyes seemed to sparkle with mischief.

Me? Trouble? No way!

She licked Lizzie on the cheek, yawned, and curled up for a nap between the two girls. Lizzie sighed contentedly. The fair had been a lot of fun—the food, the animals, the games, even the rides. But there was nothing better than a new foster puppy.

CHAPTER FOUR

At home, Lizzie let herself into the back door, quietly closing it after Waffles had slipped in behind her. "Shhh," she told the pup, holding her finger to her lips. "Remember what I promised Mom."

Lizzie had called her parents on the way home from the fair. It had taken a while to explain the situation, but finally Mom had agreed that there was nothing else to be done: Waffles had to come home with Lizzie. "But that doesn't mean we're fostering her. We'll talk about that in the morning. And remember, it's late. Your brothers are both already in bed," she said. "They'll meet Waffles in the morning, but for now please be as quiet as you can when you come in. Buddy is sleeping in Charles's room, and if you tiptoe I bet even he won't wake up."

Now, Lizzie tiptoed into the kitchen, switched on the light, and went to the cupboard to find the dog bowls her family always used for foster pups. She pulled them out, grabbed the bag of puppy food, and filled one of the bowls. She put it down for Waffles, then went to the sink to fill the other bowl with water.

Waffles followed her to the sink. "Waffles," Lizzie whispered. "Go on and eat! You must be hungry—unless people have been giving you their scraps at the fair?" She groaned, thinking about all the greasy, sugary foods the dog might have eaten. But when she turned to put down the water bowl, Waffles went to sniff at the food. She looked up at Lizzie and licked her chops.

Is this for me? What about you, aren't you hungry?

"Go ahead," Lizzie urged her. "It's all yours." She folded her arms and stood watching as Waffles ate. She didn't want to distract the puppy now that she was chowing down.

"Oh, my goodness!"

Lizzie whirled around to see Mom in the doorway in her bathrobe and p.j.'s. Her mother had spoken in a low, quiet tone, but she couldn't keep the surprise out of her voice. "She really is adorable, isn't she?"

"Told you," said Lizzie, smiling. "She's really smart, too. And playful—Buddy is going to love her."

"When he meets her—tomorrow," Mom said. "And you can tell me more about the fair then, too. And we'll discuss whether we are really going to foster this puppy. But for now, please remember what I told you about being quiet as you go upstairs."

Lizzie nodded and made the "zipping-my-lip" gesture. "Got it," she whispered, just as Waffles gobbled up the last bite of puppy kibble. "Going now." She gave her mom a hug, then patted her thigh. "Come on, Waffles," she said.

The fluffy white pup followed Lizzie right upstairs and into the bathroom where she sat watching while Lizzie brushed her teeth. Then she followed Lizzie into her bedroom and sprang right up onto the bed when Lizzie told her she could. She circled around and lay down with a little sigh. Lizzie snuggled close to Waffles and stroked her soft ears. "I know you must be missing your people," she whispered. "Maybe you feel a little bit insecure and that's why you stick so close to me. But don't worry, we'll find them.

I'm sure they're missing you even more than you miss them!"

The next morning Lizzie woke to a soft snuffling sound. Waffles was sharing her pillow, with her nose right up by Lizzie's cheek.

Good morning! I feel all fresh and happy after a good sleep. Can we go find my people now?

Lizzie rubbed her eyes. "Good morning, Waffles." She kissed the pup on the nose, then jumped out of bed. "Time to meet the rest of the family!" she said as she pulled on her bathrobe and slippers.

Waffles followed her downstairs, then into the kitchen. "Something smells good!" Lizzie said. Her stomach rumbled. How could she even be hungry after all she'd eaten at the fair? She couldn't help it. The kitchen was filled with the most delicious aroma.

"I made waffles in honor of our new guest," Dad said. He set a bottle of maple syrup on the table, then gave Lizzie a hug. "Hello, Waffles! Nice to meet you!" He hunkered down to shake the new puppy's paw. "Charles and the Bean and Buddy are all out in the backyard with Mom, waiting to get to know you."

Lizzie headed for the sliding door that led out onto the deck. "Don't worry," she told Waffles, who was right behind her. "Everybody's really nice. And Buddy loves to play."

Waffles paused for a moment at the top of the deck as if she was unsure about what to do. Then she spotted Buddy, who stood over his toy football with his tail wagging. She ran down the stairs, and they circled each other, sniffing, then took off together at a mad gallop around the yard.

"It never fails." Mom shook her head, smiling. "I don't think Buddy's ever met a puppy he didn't like."

Lizzie always thought this was one of the best things about fostering: Buddy got to meet new playmates all the time. He was so friendly and so generous with his toys. It made her love him even more.

"Look at them go!" Charles said. "She's almost as fast as he is. And—look! She just stole his football!"

The Bean laughed his googly laugh and clapped his hands. "Puppy friends!" he shouted. "Go, puppies!"

Buddy tore after Waffles and, after a brief wrestling match, got the football back. He trotted up to his family with his tail held high, proud of himself.

"Good boy, Buddy," they all said, clustering

around their puppy to pet and praise him. Charles pretended to play tug with the football while the Bean stroked Buddy's ears and Lizzie tickled the heart-shaped white patch in the middle of his chest. Mom smiled down at them. "You really are a good boy, Buddy," she said.

Lizzie straightened up. "Looks like he and Waffles will get along great." She looked around. "Wait—where is she? Where's Waffles?"

Lizzie felt her heart thumping fast. The yard wasn't that big, and there weren't many places for a fluffy white puppy to hide. Lizzie ran to the swing set and checked behind the rosebushes. "Waffles!" she cried.

There was no answer. The little white pup who had stuck so close to Lizzie since they'd met was gone now, gone without a trace.

CHAPTER FIVE

"Waffles!" Lizzie cried again.

"Waffles!" called Mom, and Charles, and the Bean.

Lizzie felt her heart pounding. How could this have happened? The yard was fenced, and the gates—one by the driveway, one by the other side of the house—were always closed and locked. Could Waffles have jumped over the fence? While the rest of her family fanned out into the yard, Lizzie ran to check the gates. The one by the driveway was closed. She dashed around the house to check the other one.

"Oh, no!" She gasped. The gate was hanging open.

Lizzie raced to the backyard. "The gate! It's open!" she shouted. "Waffles found it, and she's gone. And she's not even wearing a collar!"

"Okay," Mom said. "Let's not panic. Charles, call Buddy and get him inside. Lizzie—"

"I'm going to grab a collar and leash and some treats and go looking for her," Lizzie said. She didn't want to waste a second.

Mom nodded. "Okay. Dad can go with you. And Charles and the Bean can come with me in the van. We'll drive around the neighborhood slowly. I'm sure we'll find Waffles soon."

Lizzie took a deep breath to calm herself. She couldn't believe this was happening! Their family was always so careful to keep their foster puppies safe.

She ran up the deck stairs and went inside, heading straight for the rack by the back door where they kept spare leashes and collars. "Dad," she said as she grabbed a set. "Waffles ran off. Can you come with me to try to find her?"

"Absolutely," said Dad. He turned off the waffle iron. "Cheese?" he asked, heading for the fridge.

Lizzie nodded. She knew just what he was thinking. "Perfect," she said. Dad was right: dogs could never resist cheese. It was the best treat to have on you if you were trying to tempt a dog to come closer.

They headed out as Mom herded Charles and the Bean into the van. "Text if you find her!" Mom called.

Lizzie gave her a thumbs-up. She felt better already. Her family was a great team, and they would find Waffles—she just knew it!

Dad and Lizzie walked down the block, checking every yard. Waffles was not at the Mellerstens' next door, with their neat brick walkway leading up to their neat olive-green house. She was not at the DeZagos', the tall white house with pale blue shutters and a pool in the side yard. Lizzie peered into the Crables's backyard, where she sometimes played badminton on summer nights, with Lisa and Gracie. No Waffles.

"Waffles!" called Lizzie. "Waffles!" Then she thought of something, and her shoulders slumped. "Dad," she said, tugging on his sleeve. "That's not even her name! It's just the name we've been calling her."

Dad nodded. "I know," he said. "But from what I've heard, she really likes you. So maybe if she hears the sound of your voice she'll come running, no matter what name you call her."

"I'm going to try some other names," Lizzie said. "Who knows? Maybe I'll get the right one." She thought for a second, then put her hands around her mouth to make a megaphone. "Snowy!" she called. Maybe her people had named her after something white. Or, maybe she had a French name since poodles were originally from France. Lizzie put her hands to her mouth, then paused. "Dad, what's a French name?"

Dad, who had been looking very serious, cracked a smile. "How about Jacqueline?" he said, with a pretend French accent. "Or Mademoiselle?"

Lizzie tried both of those, even though she couldn't quite copy Dad's silly fake accent. Then, as they passed the Printzes' brick house, she decided to go back to just calling Waffles. "Waffles!" she shouted as loudly as she could. She clapped her hands. She whistled. She called again as she peered into the dense shrubbery of the Printzes' yard.

Lizzie threw up her hands. "We'll never find her," she said. "Poor Waffles. Now she'll be a stray, living on her own. What if she runs into the street and—" She couldn't even say it. She'd only known Waffles for a few hours, and already she was totally in love with her. That fluffy coat! Those sparkly eyes! That fun-loving spirit! She really was a special pup. Lizzie couldn't even imagine how her owners must feel. They hadn't seen her since last night! Lizzie stopped right there on the sidewalk and burst into tears. She couldn't help herself.

Dad pulled her in for a hug. "Come on, now," he said. "Let's not give up on her quite yet. Remember, Mom and Charles and the Bean are out looking, too. She can't have gotten that far away."

"But they haven't found her, either. They would have texted," Lizzie said into her father's warm hug. He held her closer until she stopped crying.

"Okay," she said after a moment. She sniffed and wiped her nose on her sleeve. "Let's keep on looking." She trudged on down the sidewalk, peering into yard after yard. She called Waffles's name. She called every other name she could think of. She clapped her hands. She whistled.

Nothing.

"Well," said Dad after a few more minutes. "We've made it pretty much around the block. Let's stop in at the house and see if Mom and your brothers are back."

The van wasn't in the driveway when they got home, but Dad headed toward the house, anyway. "I left my baseball cap in the backyard," he said. "I'll just grab it before we head back out." Lizzie followed him, dragging her feet.

"Hey!" Dad said as he pushed open the gate. "Would you look at that?"

"What?" Lizzie's head hung down as she stared at her sneakers. She couldn't believe they hadn't found Waffles yet.

"Lizzie!" Dad shook her shoulder, and she looked up.

There was Waffles, sitting on the back deck. She tilted her head and wagged her tail, holding up one paw as if to wave hello.

Hey there, friend! Where have you been? I've missed you!

Then she leapt off the deck and dashed straight into Lizzie's waiting arms.

CHAPTER SIX

Lizzie held Waffles tight and buried her face in the soft curls of the puppy's coat. She almost felt like crying again—this time from relief and happiness. "Waffles," she said. "That was not funny, you know." She sat back on her heels and gave the puppy a stern look.

Waffles looked back at her, with mischief in her sparkly black eyes.

Well, it was a little bit funny! I only left for a second to look for my people. What's the big deal?

Dad texted Mom to tell her the good news, then went to check the gate on the fence. "It's closed again now," he said. "But I have a feeling that this rascal figured out how to open the latch. We may have an escape artist on our hands. Maybe her real name is Houdini."

Lizzie laughed. Dad had once read her a book about Houdini, the man who could escape from anything, even if he was handcuffed inside a steel box underwater. "We'll have to keep a close eye on her."

"I'll grab a couple of bungee cords and use them to make sure that gate can't be opened if she plays with the latch," Dad said. "In fact, I'll do that to both gates. We'll just have to go through the house and use the sliding door to get in and out of the yard for the next couple of days, until—"

"Until we find your people," Lizzie told Waffles,

giving her another hug. "That's the most important thing." She looked up at Dad. "But—I don't even know where to start. Should we bring her back to the fair? Or take her to Dr. Gibson's to see if she has a microchip? Or make signs, and post on social media? What about calling all the shelters and the police?" Lizzie flopped back onto the lawn, her arms spread wide. She felt totally overwhelmed.

"Sounds like you do know where to start," said Dad. "All those are great ideas."

Lizzie sighed. "I know," she said. As Mr. Santiago had pointed out the night before, this wasn't the first time she and her family had dealt with a lost dog. She did kind of know what to do. But it would have been so much more fun to just spend the day playing in the yard with Waffles. She got up and dusted herself off. "I'll go inside and call Dr. Gibson."

Waffles sprang up, ready to follow her.

"And you," Lizzie said, shaking her finger at the puppy, "are going to be wearing a collar from now on." She held out the one she had grabbed when she and Dad went looking for Waffles. It was red with the Petersons' phone number printed on it. "If you escape again, at least someone will know who to call," Lizzie said as she clipped it on and checked the fit.

Waffles shook herself off and did a few little dance steps, glancing up at Lizzie.

Does it look cute on me?

"You look adorable," Lizzie told her. "Now, let's go call the vet. And the police. And the shelters."

Later that day, Dad and Lizzie headed off to take Waffles to see Dr. Gibson. Even though it was Sunday, her day off, the vet was always happy to help out with any puppies the Petersons were fostering.

"Well, look at you!" she said when she welcomed them into her exam room. "Aren't you a cutie-pie?" She knelt down to offer her hand to Waffles. Once Dr. Gibson was sure the puppy felt comfortable with her, she petted her softly, touching her all over. "She's certainly been well cared for," the vet said as she pulled out her stethoscope. She listened to the puppy's heart and lungs for a moment, then told Lizzie and Dad that Waffles was perfectly healthy. "Obviously she hasn't been on her own for long. She's well-fed and nicely groomed."

"That's what I thought," said Lizzie. "I think she just ran off at the fair. We're going back there after this to look for her owners again."

"Let's just check if she has been microchipped," said Dr. Gibson. She pulled a scanner out of a drawer and ran it over the puppy.

"I don't hear any beeping," said Lizzie. She had a feeling that wasn't a good sign.

Dr. Gibson shook her head. "Too bad," she said. "We could have had her back with her people right away if she was chipped." She ruffled Waffles's floppy ears. "But I'm sure these nice folks will help you find your way home anyway," she told the puppy.

Waffles gazed up at the vet and wagged her tail.

Thanks for helping!

Then she pranced out of the office at the end of the leash that Lizzie held, ready for whatever came next.

A little later, Dad pulled into the grassy parking lot at the county fair and they piled out of the van, Lizzie holding tight to Waffles's leash. "Wow," she said as they walked over the bridge from the parking lot to the fairgrounds. "It sure looks different during the day." There were no colored lights on the midway. Some of the stalls had already been taken down. And only a few people strolled here and there, taking one last chance to win a stuffie or buy a T-shirt.

"The last day of the fair is always kind of sad," Dad said. "I remember that from other years." He waved a hand around at the midway. "All these people are packing up to go to the next fair in the next place. The animals are mostly back at their home farms, and the rides are being taken down."

"Fine with me," muttered Lizzie. If she never had to go on another ride in her life, she'd be happy.

Waffles pulled at the leash, eager to check out the sights and smells. "Where are we going, Waffles?" Lizzie asked. She turned to Dad. "I wonder if she's looking for her people. Maybe I should let her decide which way we go."

But Waffles seemed to be taking a random

route. She went by the big barn where the pony pull had been held, then stopped for a moment near a chili-dog food truck, sniffing. After that, she pulled Lizzie along to a big, empty parking lot at the other end of the midway, the one where people unloaded large animals. Then she pulled back, toward the animal barns.

Lizzie sighed. "She's just checking everything out," she said. "And nobody's checking her out. We might as well head home."

"Let's just stop at the fair offices first," Dad suggested. This time, a woman opened the door when they knocked. She smiled and asked what she could do for them. She took their phone number and promised to make a few announcements over the loudspeaker. "But," she said, "there aren't many folks here anymore. I wouldn't get your hopes up."

CHAPTER SEVEN

"That wasn't very encouraging," said Maria later that day. She had come over to help Lizzie make LOST DOG signs—or rather, FOUND DOG signs—and Lizzie had just told her about what the woman at the fair had said. "What about the fair's social media? Can't this lady post something there?"

"Well, the thing is," Lizzie said as she laid out markers and poster board, "she can't. She doesn't know how. She said that her coworker Sheila does. But Sheila won't be in till tomorrow."

"Frustrating," said Maria. She glanced down at

Waffles, who, as always, was sitting inches away from Lizzie. "You just know somebody is really missing this dog."

"And she's missing them, too," Lizzie said. She picked an orange marker to outline the red letters she'd made. IS THIS YOUR DOG? her sign said. They had already taken pictures of Waffles and printed them out on Mom's printer. They planned to stick the pictures (which were adorable) to the poster board, above the necessary information, like the Petersons' phone number. "I think that's why she clings to me the way she does. Somehow she's decided that I'm her safe place. She wants to be close to me all the time."

"Except when she runs off," Maria said. Lizzie had told her all about Waffles getting out of the fenced backyard.

"Oh, please! Don't remind me," said Lizzie.

"Believe me, I haven't let her out of my sight since then. And she's always wearing a collar, and I've always got her on a leash when we leave the house. Houdini or not, she's never getting away again." She bent over to ruffle Waffles's soft ears. The puppy's curly white coat was so soft! "Right, Waffles?"

Waffles thumped her tail and shook her head so her ears flippy-flopped.

Sure, whatever you say . . . unless I get a good chance to go find my people!

"I guess she must have run off that time to try to find her people," Maria said. "But they could be anywhere! People come from all over to go to the fair."

"What I don't get is why they would have left the fair without their dog in the first place," Lizzie said. "It just doesn't make sense. Why would anyone leave this cutie behind?" She smiled down at Waffles. "I mean, she's the perfect puppy. She's cute, she's full of energy, she's really smart, and she's funny. She makes me laugh all the time."

As if on cue, Waffles rolled over onto her back, paws in the air. Her pink belly shone as she squirmed happily, rubbing her back on the carpet.

How about a tummy rub? It's been ages since the last one.

Lizzie and Maria looked at each other and laughed, then got down on the floor with Waffles to give her all the pets and belly rubs she wanted.

Once the signs were finished, after many more breaks for tummy rubs and puppy fun, Lizzie and

Maria got ready to head out to put them up. "Dad said he'll take a couple of signs over to the fairgrounds," Lizzie said, "but I don't know if it's even worth it. The fair is basically over after today, and everyone has pretty much packed up and left by now."

"It can't hurt," said Maria. "We should just put them up everywhere. But I guess we should start downtown, right?"

"Sounds like a plan," said Lizzie as she snapped a leash onto the white puppy's collar. "What do you think, Waffles?" Waffles pranced around in the hallway, ready for adventure.

I'll go anywhere with you! Is my friend Buddy coming, too?

Buddy, who had just woken from a nap, looked at Lizzie hopefully. "Not this time, Bud," said

Lizzie. "I want to make sure my full attention is on Waffles so she doesn't get away from me again. We'll have some playtime out back when we get home."

Buddy hung his head, then trotted back to the couch for more napping.

The girls headed toward downtown with Waffles at Lizzie's side. The puppy was interested in everything they passed: bushes, mailboxes, and flowerpots all got examined and sniffed. She seemed to notice everything; her bright eyes took it all in, and Lizzie could practically see her learning about the neighborhood. Or—was she still looking for her own neighborhood?

When they got downtown, Lizzie knew just what their first stop should be: her favorite store, Lucky Dog Books. Jerry, the owner, was always happy to greet any dogs who came by. He kept a canister of dog treats on the counter, left water bowls outside on hot days, and had a basket of dog toys in a corner.

"Well, well, well, who's this?" he asked, coming around the counter to say hello to Waffles. Lizzie let go of the leash, knowing that dogs were safe in this store.

She and Maria explained about finding Waffles at the fair. "Well, it wasn't so much that we found her as that she found us," Lizzie said.

"She's a dear," said Jerry. "I'm sure somebody is missing her very much."

"That's why we wanted to ask if we could put this poster up in your window," said Lizzie. She showed him what they'd made.

"Absolutely," said Jerry. "And if you have extra, I'll post some around my neighborhood." He stood to get Lizzie some tape, then knelt back down to play with Waffles. Lizzie went to the front of the store to put up the poster from the inside, facing out. She was just sticking on the last piece of tape when the bell over the front door rang as a customer came in.

"Grab the leash!" Lizzie turned to shout to Jerry and Maria. But before anyone could move, she saw a white blur race past and slip outside the door, just as it swung closed.

Waffles had escaped—again!

CHAPTER EIGHT

"Oh, nooo!" Lizzie groaned. She threw down the tape dispenser and flew out the door after Waffles. She looked to her right. No Waffles. And to her left: no Waffles! How could one puppy disappear so fast? Lizzie's heart was racing. What should she do? Run down the sidewalk toward the post office? Or toward the rec fields? She had no way of knowing which way Waffles had gone. Lizzie took some deep breaths, trying to calm herself so she could think.

The bell on the door jingled and Maria and Jerry ran out. "Did you see her?" Maria asked. "Which way did she go?"

Lizzie held up her hands. "I don't know," she said.

"I'm so, so sorry that I didn't grab her leash in time," said Jerry. "She took off like a racehorse before I had a second to think."

Lizzie shook her head. "It's not your fault. It's mine. I never should have let go of her leash in the first place."

"At least she has a collar on this time," Maria said. "And it has your phone number on it. Maybe somebody will catch her and see that."

Lizzie nodded, but she was hardly hearing what Maria was saying. Her thoughts were a jumble. How were they going to find Waffles?

Jerry put his hands on her shoulders. "Don't worry, Lizzie. We'll find her." He stepped inside and switched the sign on the door to read CLOSED. "You girls go that way," he said, pointing to the right. "I'll go the other way. How far could she have gotten? Just do me a favor and stay on the sidewalk.

Even if you see her in the street, don't go running after her."

"That doesn't work, anyway," Lizzie said. She was beginning to feel a little calmer. "If you run after dogs, they just think it's a game of chase. They'll run even faster. The best thing to do is run the other way or pretend you're seeing something really interesting on the ground. They get curious and come right to you." Lizzie had done this with Buddy a zillion times, and it always worked.

Jerry nodded. "Good advice," he said. "I'll remember that." He held up his phone. "I'll call your mom and dad and let them know what's happening—just in case they get a call from someone who catches Waffles."

Lizzie nodded. "Okay," she said, even though she hated to have her parents know she had messed up so badly by letting go of that leash.

"Come on," said Maria. She grabbed Lizzie's hand. "Let's get going. Hopefully she hasn't gotten far."

They headed down the street toward the rec fields. As they trotted along, Lizzie scanned the sidewalks on both sides, watching for a flash of white. She saw all kinds of people, and several dogs, but Waffles was nowhere in sight.

"We'll find her." Maria squeezed Lizzie's hand. "I just know it."

Lizzie wished she felt so sure. She just didn't get it. Why was Waffles so clingy most of the time—then off like a rocket other times? "Maybe she smelled something," Lizzie said, thinking out loud. "You know how dogs have such an incredible sense of smell, like ten thousand times what we have? What if her people were nearby and she could smell them?" She panted as she spoke, since she and Maria were still trotting down the sidewalk.

"Maybe," said Maria. "Or maybe she just likes to run away sometimes. Like you told me your Dad said: she's a Houdini dog." Maria was panting, too.

Lizzie kept scanning, moving her head from left to right, looking everywhere. "Waffles!" she called, even though it was probably no use. "Waffles, where are you?"

As they left the downtown area, heading for the rec fields, there were fewer parked cars and it was easier to see everything. But now cars were moving faster as they passed, and Lizzie felt a chill run down her spine. "What if Waffles sees us and runs toward us, across the street?" she asked Maria.

Maria frowned. "She won't," she said. "She's too smart for that."

"Being smart doesn't mean she understands about cars," said Lizzie. "Unless her owners have taught her." She had taught Buddy to sit right next to her when they were walking together and she said, "Car!" She had also taught him the emergency "down." No matter where he was, how far away from her, if she held her hand high and shouted, "Buddy, down!" Buddy would drop instantly. It worked whether he was across the yard, across the dog park, or across a street.

But she had no idea whether Waffles would do the same. She really didn't know Waffles at all, she realized. They hadn't even spent twenty-four hours together yet. Lizzie felt a stab in her gut. It hadn't even been twenty-four hours, and she'd lost this puppy twice!

She groaned and held her stomach.

"What is it?" asked Maria. "Are you sick? Lizzie?" She stopped and put an arm around Lizzie's shoulders.

"No, I'm okay," said Lizzie. "I just can't believe

I have let this puppy out of my sight—twice!—in such a short time. I mean, should I even be fostering puppies?"

Maria laughed. "Oh, Lizzie, come on. It could happen to anyone! You know you're the best friend and protector any dog could ever have."

Lizzie gave Maria a little smile. "Really?" she asked. Her legs felt shaky.

"Really," said Maria. "Now, let's find that puppy!"

As they neared the rec fields, Lizzie saw three people on horseback riding out of the woods. Everyone used those trails: dog walkers, skiers, runners, bikers. But she'd never seen people on horses before. It looked like a whole group had been riding together.

Then, just ahead of them, parked on the side of the road, she saw a few horse trailers, the kind pulled by pickup trucks. People were leading horses into them, calling good-byes to their friends.

As they got closer, Lizzie saw one of the truck doors open. Somebody leaned out, reaching for—

"Waffles!" Lizzie cried. "Dognappers! No! Leave her alone!" She flew toward the truck with Maria right on her heels. Would they get there in time?

CHAPTER NINE

"Lizzie, wait!" Maria grabbed Lizzie by the sleeve. "What are you doing? You can't just go charging up to people like that."

"But—but—" Lizzie tried to pull away. "They're taking Waffles!"

Maria held on tighter. "If they *are* dognappers, that's even worse. I'm not going to let you run straight up to some criminals."

"You're absolutely right, Maria."

Lizzie turned to see her dad standing there, shaking his head. "I know you love puppies, but you've got to take care of yourself first if you want to keep taking care of them," he said. "Jerry called me, and I came right over to help."

Lizzie let out a breath, and her shoulders sagged. "But Dad, we can't let them take her away! We have to find her people."

Dad raised his eyebrows. "Maybe those people in the pickup *are* her people!" he said.

"I didn't even think of that."

"At least they haven't driven off yet," said Maria. The horse trailer and pickup were still parked nearby. The door of the pickup was closed, and Waffles was nowhere in sight.

"Stay here," Dad told Maria and Lizzie. "I'm going to go talk to them."

"Ha," said Lizzie. "As if." There was no way she was going to stay put.

Dad rolled his eyes. "Okay, then, let's go. Just stay behind me in case they are dangerous. Which

I'm pretty sure they're not." He led the way to the passenger side of the pickup and knocked on the window.

The woman in the front seat rolled it down—and Waffles stuck her head out and shook her ears, giving them a happy doggy grin.

Hey, I've been wondering where you went!

Dad introduced himself. "I hate to bother you, but I'm just wondering—is that your dog?"

The woman laughed. "I wish!" she said. "What a darling. She just jumped into the truck to say hi, and we've been cuddling ever since. Is she yours?"

Dad explained that they'd found her as a stray and were fostering her. "She—uh, she's a very talented escape artist," he said.

Lizzie knew that Dad was trying to make her

feel better. "It's my fault she ran away," she said. "I should have been watching her more carefully."

"Well, anyway, I'm glad somebody's looking after her," said the woman. She climbed out of the truck, helping Waffles out as well. Lizzie grabbed the leash the puppy was still trailing and held on tight. Waffles leaned against her knee, and Lizzie gave her a scratch between the ears.

"I hope you find her people soon," said the woman. She paused. "You know, now that I think of it, she seems kind of familiar. Can I get your number? I'll call you if I think of anything."

They gave her the number and said good-bye. "Come on, I'll give you a ride home," Dad said to Lizzie and Maria as they walked away with Waffles. Lizzie held the leash as tightly as she could, wrapping it twice around her wrist.

Lizzie climbed into the backseat next to Maria and Waffles and plopped down, heaving a huge sigh. "I give up." She buried her face in the puppy's soft fur. "I don't have a clue what to do next."

"That doesn't sound like the Lizzie I know," Dad said from the front seat.

"Sure doesn't," said Maria. "Come on. It's like my riding teacher, Kathy, always tells me when I'm trying something hard and I want to quit. 'Just give it one more go—and then another!' Sometimes you just have to keep trying, even if you think something is impossible."

Lizzie nodded, but she wasn't really listening. Her mind had taken off in a different direction when Maria mentioned her riding teacher. "Horses!" she said.

Maria stared at her. "Um—what?"

"Maybe Waffles is interested in horses," Lizzie said. "Maybe that's why she went to those people with the trailer. And maybe she smelled a horse the other day when she took off from my house. And . . . now that I think of it, she was checking out all the horsey places at the fair earlier today!"

"Uh-huh," said Maria, giving Lizzie a bewildered look. "And?"

"And so maybe her owners are horse people!" Lizzie said. "I'm sure all the horse people from around here were at the fair." She leaned forward in her seat. "Dad, can you take us to Kathy's stable? Maybe she can help." Lizzie felt energized by her new idea. Maybe it would come to nothing— but at least it was an idea.

"Now?" Dad asked.

"Yup!" said Lizzie. She sat back in her seat, smiling as she gave Waffles a kiss on the nose. She felt better already.

"Now, that's the Lizzie I *do* know," said Maria, laughing.

Kathy greeted them warmly when they arrived. "And oh, my gosh, who's this adorable pup?" She bent down to pet Waffles.

"Hmm, that's a tough one," Kathy said when they'd told her about finding Waffles at the fair, and how she was lost—or her people were!—and how she seemed interested in horses. "You know, I don't travel much from my own barn, so I don't know lots of the folks who go to the fair with their horses." Kathy tapped her lip, thinking. "Tell you what, I'll give you Jamie's number. I think she does some of the jumping events at the fair with her horse. And Jim's number, too—he's a farrier, so he knows all the horses around here."

Lizzie gave Maria a questioning look. She had no idea what a farrier was. Maria smiled. "Kind of like a blacksmith," she explained. "He goes around to all the barns to shoe horses and ponies."

"And here's Stacey's number, and Alex's." Kathy scribbled on a scrap of paper. "Horse people. Who knows? Maybe one of them will have an idea for you about where this cutie belongs." She bent to pet Waffles, who had been waiting patiently while the humans talked. The puppy's nose was working overtime, sniffing the air all around, and her bright eyes kept watch on the barn where Kathy's students boarded their horses.

This place seems so familiar—but it's not my home. Where are my people?

"Don't worry, Waffles," said Lizzie. "We are going to find them."

CHAPTER TEN

But they didn't. They did not find the puppy's owners at Windrush Stables or at the Tanglewood Riding Center. They got no leads from the farrier, or from the jumping teacher named Dave, or from Jason, who ran the pony rides at Shelley's Petting Zoo. Everyone wanted to help—especially once they'd met Waffles—but nobody was able to.

"Poor Waffles." Lizzie sighed as Dad drove home after they'd dropped off Maria.

"She doesn't seem too upset at the moment," Dad said, meeting Lizzie's eyes in the rearview mirror.

Waffles sat up elegantly on the backseat,

watching out the window as they drove through the neighborhood. Her tongue hung out, she grinned that special "riding-in-a-car" grin that some dogs have, and her little tail wagged and wagged as she took in the sights.

Look! That's a big tree. I bet there are tons of squirrels up in there. Whee! What fun!

"She doesn't seem to let it get her down that we can't find her people," said Lizzie, ruffling the puppy's soft curly coat. "She's just happy by nature, I guess."

"And she feels safe with you," said Dad.

That made Lizzie feel warm all over. That's all she ever wanted: for the puppies she cared for to feel safe and happy. "She is," said Lizzie. "She's very safe, especially now that I never, ever, ever let go of this leash when we are out of the house."

She held up her arm to show Dad the leash wrapped twice around her wrist.

"Mom, please?" Lizzie begged the next morning. "How can I go to school and leave Waffles behind? I'm, like, her security blanket!"

Mom shook her head, arms crossed. "Not going to happen," she said. "Waffles will just have to put up with me today. I promise to give her lots of attention and—"

"Never, ever let go of the leash!" Lizzie finished. She knelt to give Waffles a hug and kiss good-bye. "I'll be back as soon as I can," she told the puppy. "And then I'll get right back to work on trying to find your people."

But Lizzie didn't forget about Waffles, not for a second. Lizzie doodled poodle pictures in her notebook during math class. At free reading time she ignored her book and instead made a list of all the possible names she could think of for a white poodle puppy. And during computer time she researched standard poodles to try to figure out more about Waffles and her personality.

And now, when she was supposed to be working on her geography project—a 3D map of Brazil—she was jotting down reminders for herself instead. *Call Dr. Gibson again,* she wrote. *Check in with police. Put up more posters.*

"Lizzie?"

She looked up to see her teacher Ms. Abeson, motioning her to come to the front of the room. "I just had a text from the principal's office," she said. "They have a message for you. I think they want you to call your mom."

Lizzie's heart rose. "Maybe it's something about Waffles," she said. She'd told all about the puppy and her adventures during sharing time.

Ms. Abeson smiled. "Head on down and find out what's up," she said.

A few minutes later, Lizzie shouted into the phone, "What? That's amazing!" Mom had just told her the big news: Some people who claimed that Waffles belonged to them had called just a few minutes earlier. They were on their way to pick her up! "So when are you coming to get me?" Lizzie asked. There was no way she was going to miss this.

"They won't be here for quite a while," Mom told her. "They each have a long way to drive."

"From where?" Lizzie asked. "Who are they? How do we know that Waffles really belongs to them?"

"It's a long story," Mom said. "You'll hear about it when you get home—*after* school. Bye!" She hung up before Lizzie could protest.

Lizzie couldn't pay attention to a thing for

the rest of the day. All she did was think about Waffles and watch the clock, waiting for school to be over. She had so many questions!

As soon as the last bell rang, Lizzie dashed out the doors. She jumped on her bike and rode home as fast as she could.

There was no car parked in front of the house. No sign of any visitors. Was that good? Or was it bad? Maybe they had already come and taken Waffles away! Lizzie held her breath as she pushed open the front door, then let it out in a happy sigh when she saw Waffles running toward her. "Yay!" she said, kneeling to open her arms to the pup. "You're still here."

Waffles wriggled with joy, and shook her ears, and wagged her tail, and licked Lizzie's cheek.

I'm so happy to see you! I thought you went away forever!

When Lizzie looked up, Mom was smiling down at her. "Get your hugs in now," she said. "I have a feeling we'll have company very soon."

"But who?" Lizzie asked. "Who are her people?"

"Well, they were at the fair—" Mom began. But just then, they both heard something outside.

Lizzie ran to the window. "It's them!" she said. "Wow, *two* pickup trucks hauling *two* trailers."

"Exactly," Mom said. "Sarah, that's the wife— she works with ponies."

"I saw her! I saw her at the fair!" Lizzie yelled. This was too exciting. The woman getting out of the truck was the one who had won the blue ribbon at the pony pull. Lizzie recognized her right away.

"And Jackson, her husband, works with oxen," Mom finished. "They both had to leave our fair in a big hurry—Sarah was headed to another fair in Maine, and Jackson had one in New Hampshire. Each of them thought that the other one had

Waffles. They only realized their mistake after their events were over and they had a second to catch their breath and listen to their phone messages."

"Wow," said Lizzie.

"Their phones were totally lighting up," said Mom. "All of that asking around you did really paid off: There were messages from all sorts of people, letting them know their dog was safe with us. Horse people, fair people, a whole network of folks. It's like they say, it takes a village. A lot of people working together can really accomplish something—and you're the one who got them all working on it," Mom finished, smiling at Lizzie. "You did well, Lizzie."

Lizzie ducked her head. "Thanks," she said. "But—are we positive that Waffles belongs to them? How can they prove it?"

There was a knock on the door before Mom

could answer. When she opened it, Waffles flew out of Lizzie's arms and galloped straight toward the couple who stood on the porch. Both people burst into tears as they caught the puppy in their arms for a group hug.

"Oh, Francine," said Sarah. "My baby!"

"You little rascal," Jackson said as he kissed the puppy's nose. "How did you escape this time?" He shook his head and looked up at Lizzie and Mom, wiping his eyes. "This one is a real Houdini."

Lizzie burst out laughing. She and Mom exchanged a look. They had all the proof they needed. Waffles—Francine!—definitely knew these people, and they knew her.

Then Lizzie realized something: She was going to have to say good-bye. Her laughter was replaced by tears. She shook her head, trying to clear the sadness away. "You'll—you'll get her microchipped, right?" she asked. "And keep her on a leash?"

Sarah and Jackson nodded. "Oh, you bet we will," said Sarah. She smiled down at the white pup and ruffled her ears. "No more running away for you, young lady."

Lizzie sniffed, wiped her tears on her sleeve, and tried to smile as she knelt down for one last hug. As much as she was going to miss this very special pup, Lizzie was happy to know that she was going home.

PUPPY TIPS

If your dog ever gets lost, there's lots you can do to try to find them. Get the word out: Put up as many posters as you can, and call your local animal shelters and the police. Check out all the places where you've spent time together, and remember to keep good treats in your pockets when you go searching! Your parents can help you use social media as well.

And most importantly, Dr. Gibson's advice was good: Get your dog microchipped! It saves a lot of time and energy if a lost dog can be identified right away.

Dear Reader,

I feel very lucky that my dog, Zipper, has never run off for long. I would be so upset if that happened! He is microchipped, so hopefully he would be returned to me quickly. But if he ran off into the woods and got lost, I don't know how I would ever find him. That's why I keep him on a leash unless we are in very familiar, safe areas like my backyard or the trails we walk daily. I also carry a whistle for calling him and treats to reward him when he comes. That way, he never wanders far.

Yours from the Puppy Place,

Ellen Miles

THE PUPPY PLACE

**For another book about a
lost puppy, try** BIGGIE **or** ZIGGY!

ABOUT THE AUTHOR

Ellen Miles loves dogs, which is why she has a great time writing the Puppy Place books. And guess what? She loves cats, too! (In fact, her very first pet was a beautiful tortoiseshell cat named Jenny.) That's why she came up with the Kitty Corner series. Ellen lives in Vermont and loves to be outdoors with her dog, Zipper, every day, walking, biking, skiing, or swimming, depending on the season. She also loves to read, cook, explore her beautiful state, play with dogs, and hang out with friends and family.

Visit Ellen at ellenmiles.net.